Dear Parents:

Congratulations! Your child is taking the first steps on an exciting journey. The destination? Independent reading!

STEP INTO READING® will help your child get there. The program offers five steps to reading success. Each step includes fun stories and colorful art or photographs. In addition to original fiction and books with favorite characters, there are Step into Reading Non-Fiction Readers, Phonics Readers and Boxed Sets, Sticker Readers, and Comic Readers—a complete literacy program with something to interest every child.

Learning to Read, Step by Step!

Ready to Read Preschool–Kindergarten
• big type and easy words • rhyme and rhythm • picture clues
For children who know the alphabet and are eager to begin reading.

Reading with Help Preschool–Grade 1
• basic vocabulary • short sentences • simple stories
For children who recognize familiar words and sound out new words with help.

Reading on Your Own Grades 1–3
• engaging characters • easy-to-follow plots • popular topics
For children who are ready to read on their own.

Reading Paragraphs Grades 2–3
• challenging vocabulary • short paragraphs • exciting stories
For newly independent readers who read simple sentences with confidence.

Ready for Chapters Grades 2–4
• chapters • longer paragraphs • full-color art
For children who want to take the plunge into chapter books but still like colorful pictures.

STEP INTO READING® is designed to give every child a successful reading experience. The grade levels are only guides; children will progress through the steps at their own speed, developing confidence in their reading.

Remember, a lifetime love of reading starts with a single step!

★ American Girl®

Stories
of
Bravery!

The Nez Perce words that appear in Kaya's story are spelled so that English readers can pronounce them.

Nimíipuu (nee-MEE-poo) means **the People**
(known today as the Nez Perce)

Eetsa (EET-sah) means **mother**

Toe-ta (TOH-tah) means **father**

Aalah (AA-lah) means **grandmother** (on father's side)

The works in this collection were originally published separately in the United States by Random House Books for Young Readers as *Freedom for Addy* in 2021, *Kaya Rides to the Rescue* in 2022, *Melody Lifts Her Voice* in 2022, *Molly's Christmas Surprise* in 2021, and *Samantha Helps a Friend* in 2021.

Step into Reading, Random House, and the Random House colophon are registered trademarks of Penguin Random House LLC.

rhcbooks.com

Educators and librarians, for a variety of teaching tools, visit us at RHTeachersLibrarians.com

ISBN 978-0-593-64858-2 (trade)

MANUFACTURED IN CHINA

10 9 8 7 6 5 4 3 2 1

STEP 3
READING ON YOUR OWN

STEP INTO READING®

☆ American Girl®

Stories
of
Bravery!

Molly
• 1944 •

Melody
• 1964 •

Kaya
• 1764 •

Random House 🏠 New York

Contents

★ American Girl®

Freedom for Addy

by Tonya Leslie

illustrated by Tanisha Cherislin

Random House 🏠 New York

It is 1864, during the Civil War.

Addy and her family live on

a plantation in North Carolina.

They are enslaved

and considered property.

They work all day.

They do not get paid.

It's a hard life.

At bedtime, Addy, brother Sam,
and baby Esther sleep
on the floor of their small cabin.
Addy hears Momma and Poppa
whisper in the dark about
freedom . . . and running away.
Addy listens and wonders
what will happen.
Escape attempts are punished.

The next day, Addy hears
the plantation owner talking.
He says Sam and Poppa
are going to be sold.
Addy's family will be separated!
She rushes to warn them.

Addy almost spills the water

in her hurry to reach them.

"Girl," the owner yells.

"Watch yourself."

He heads to the field.

Addy's heart races with fear.

Addy is too late!

Poppa and Sam are being loaded

onto a wagon.

Their hands are bound.

Addy drops the bucket.

She runs to them,

but the owner stops her.

He shoves her back.

Addy falls into her mother's arms.

"Stop crying!" the owner growls.

"Get back to work!"

Addy's heart is breaking.

Addy and her mother

have no choice.

They must return to work.

That night, the cabin feels empty
without Poppa and Sam.
"We are not safe here,"
Momma says. "We must run!
But we can't take baby Esther."
Esther can't walk yet, and
her crying could give them away.

Addy's auntie and uncle help.

They dress Addy like a boy.

Momma is dressed like a man.

Uncle Solomon gives Addy a dime.

"Freedom's got a cost," he says.

Addy kisses baby Esther goodbye.

Momma and Addy move quickly.

They are headed north to freedom.

The forest is dark and scary.

They stumble through the trees.

After a long while, they find

a small cave to shelter in.

Addy is tired and misses her family.

Momma takes out a small shell.

"This shell belonged to your great-grandma," says Momma.

"She brought it from Africa."

Momma puts the shell on a string and around Addy's neck.

Addy knows she must be brave like her great-grandma.

Addy and Momma travel by night

so they won't get caught.

One night, their path ends at a river.

They must cross it,

but Momma can't swim.

Addy and Momma get into
the cold river.
Momma slips!
Her head goes under.
Addy reaches for her
and pulls her to shore.

"You saved me, Addy,"
Momma says weakly.
"You are a brave girl."

Momma and Addy go far away,
as fast as they can. At last,
a small house comes into view.
Is it safe? They knock and wait.

A woman named Miss Caroline
invites them in
and gives them food and new clothes.
She wants them to be free.
In the morning, Addy and her momma
will have to hide in a wagon
to continue the journey to freedom.

The wagon takes them to a boat.

The boat takes them

to Philadelphia.

The big city is a sea

of strangers.

The streets are full
of people and wagons.
It's all unfamiliar.
Addy and Momma do not know
how to read the signs.
They cannot trust strangers.
They must wait for help.

29

New friends help them get settled.
A girl named Sarah and her mother
walk Addy and Momma
to the church for aid.

Sarah's mother helps them
find a place to live.
It is small but cozy.
Momma will have to work hard
at her new job sewing clothes,
but at least she will get paid.

One day, Addy gets good news.

She will be going to school!

She will finally learn to read!

Addy is nervous

on the first day of school.

Will she make friends?

One girl makes friends
with Addy right away.
It's Sarah, the girl Addy met
the day she arrived.

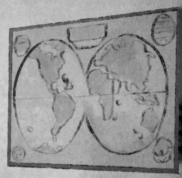

The holidays come.

Addy's momma works all the time.

Addy wants to give

her mother a gift.

She considers

using the dime from Uncle Solomon

to buy a red scarf.

Instead, she makes a scarf

with scrap fabric.

Addy gives the dime

to the church to help

other enslaved people escape.

It is Christmas Day.

Addy gives Momma

the scarf that she made.

Momma loves the present!

She has a gift for Addy, too.

It is a rag doll stuffed with beans.

"I'll call her Ida Bean," Addy says.

Later that night at church,
there is a surprise for Addy . . .

It's Poppa!

He has found them!

It's the best holiday surprise.

Addy hopes she will soon see

her brother and sister again, too.

☆ American Girl®
Kaya
Rides to the Rescue

by Emma Carlson Berne
illustrated by Emma Gillette
Based on a story by Janet Shaw

Random House 🏠 New York

Kaya rides into the river valley.

The sun sparkles on the water.

Kaya's family has come to fish

for salmon.

The year is 1764.

Kaya is part of the

Nimíipuu people—the Nez Perce.

Kaya loves nature and

the beauty of this special place.

She has a horse named Steps High.

She loves to ride fast!

Kaya has a special bond
with her horse.
Steps High comes
when Kaya whistles.
Kaya's best friend is
Speaking Rain.
Speaking Rain is blind.
Kaya and Steps High
gently lead Speaking Rain
on her horse.

Speaking Rain lives with
Kaya's family. Kaya and
Speaking Rain are like sisters.
Brown Deer is Kaya's big sister.

Kaya helps take care of
her twin brothers,
Wing Feather and Sparrow.
They love to hide, and
sometimes, they don't listen.
Kaya's mother, Eetsa, often
asks Kaya to watch the boys.

Kaya's grandmother, Aalah,

is waiting to welcome the family

when they ride up.

Kaya's father, Toe-ta,

her sister Brown Deer,

and the others

help untie the bundles and

bring them into the tepee.

Eetsa says Kaya and Speaking Rain

can take the twins to play.

She reminds Kaya to watch them.

Kaya promises she will.

A boy named Fox Tail
teases Kaya. He says Steps High
is not very fast. Kaya boasts
that Steps High is fast.
"She's as fast as an eagle!"
Kaya says.
"Let's race!" Fox Tail replies.
Kaya asks Speaking Rain
to take care of the twins,
even though that's Kaya's job.

The horse race is on!

Kaya is worried.

Steps High has not raced before.

Kaya wishes she hadn't boasted.

The horses leap forward.

Kaya pushes Steps High to go

faster and faster. Suddenly,

Steps High rears and bucks!

Kaya slides off and calms Steps High.

She knows it was wrong

to race her young horse.

Still, Kaya wishes she had won.

She challenges Fox Tail

to a race on foot.

Fox Tail runs far ahead.

Kaya is alone. She is not sure

which way to go.

She hears birds caw.

They seem to say, "Forgot! Forgot!"

Then Kaya remembers the twins!

She promised Eetsa to watch them.

Kaya runs back toward the river

as fast as she can.

Speaking Rain sits by the river.

She tells Kaya that the boys

ran away from her.

Now she can't find them.

Kaya's heart pounds.

They could fall into the river!

Kaya and Speaking Rain

search along the river and in the woods.

They find the boys up in a tree.

The boys are safe, but Kaya's auntie

saw what happened.

Kaya is in trouble.

Kaya was selfish, Auntie says.

She forgot her brothers,

so all the children

will be punished.

This will remind them

that what one person does

affects everyone.

Fox Tail calls Kaya "Magpie,"

after the selfish bird that

snatches what it wants.

It thinks only of itself.

While making dinner, Kaya tells
Aalah about her mistake. How can
she lose her awful nickname, Magpie?
Kaya should think of her brothers'
safety before her own fun,
Aalah says. She can work
with Steps High to earn the trust
of her horse and family again.
Maybe then, she will lose her nickname.

In the morning, Kaya and Toe-ta
train Steps High.
Kaya is calm and quiet,
so Steps High stays
calm and quiet as well.

Fox Tail rides up to Kaya.

He wants to race again.

This time, Kaya says no.

Steps High is not ready to race.

Fox Tail calls her Magpie

and rides off!

Kaya trains Steps High each day.

She teaches Steps High

to trust her.

She thinks about her nickname

and what she must do to get rid of it.

The salmon-fishing season ends.

The family is packing up.

Aalah can't find her special knife.

Kaya offers to look for it
near the riverbank.

Speaking Rain comes, too.

Speaking Rain says she will
search along the bushes.
Kaya searches farther downstream.
Speaking Rain moves too close
to the riverbank.
Suddenly, Kaya sees Speaking Rain
tumble into the river!

Kaya gallops Steps High
along the river.
Speaking Rain is struggling
in the rushing water.
Kaya must reach her.
"Trust me," she tells her horse.
Steps High wades into the water.
Kaya reaches Speaking Rain.
She pulls her onto Steps High.

They return to the riverbank, safe.

Toe-ta helps Speaking Rain

off the horse. He saw what happened.

Toe-ta tells Kaya she did well.

She earned Steps High's trust.

She raced to help Speaking Rain,

instead of racing to win.

"Good job, Kaya," says Fox Tail.

He calls Kaya by her name,

instead of Magpie.

Kaya hugs Steps High.

"Thank you," she whispers.

Kaya's family leaves the valley.
She rides Steps High out
to help herd the other horses.
She is proud to do her work
for her people.
Kaya will not be Magpie anymore!

☆ **American Girl®**

Melody
Lifts Her Voice

by Bria Alston

illustrated by Parker-Nia Gordon
and Shiane Salabie

Based on a story by Denise Lewis Patrick

Random House 🏠 New York

Meet Melody Ellison!

Melody is a ten-year-old girl

who lives in Detroit in 1964.

She loves to sing and garden.

She has two sisters,

a brother who is a musician,

and a dog named Bo.

On New Year's Eve, Melody attends
Watch Night service at church
with her parents, sisters,
and grandparents,
Big Momma and Poppa.

Melody and her friends
and family call church
their "home away from home."

Before the service begins,

Melody's cousin Val whispers,

"It's almost your birthday!"

Melody grins as the service starts.

"Good evening, friends!"

Pastor Daniels says.

"Good evening!" everyone calls back.
Pastor Daniels invites everybody
to pick one thing they want
to change for the better
in the coming year,
right here in their community.

After the service, families eat cake
and drink punch in the church hall.
Melody's big sister Yvonne
shares her idea to make change.

She will teach kids
about Black history and civil rights
over the summer. Melody thinks
about Pastor Daniels's message.
How can *she* make
a difference?

The next day is Melody's birthday!

At her party, everyone cheers,

"Happy birthday, Melody!"

Melody misses her brother, Dwayne.

He is away, touring with his band.

"Happy birthday to you,

my kid sister, Dee-Dee!"

sings a voice at the door.

"Dwayne!" Melody shouts.

She is surprised and so happy!

A week later, the adults in Melody's neighborhood gather for a meeting. The kids hear them talk about how unfairly Fieldston's clothing store has treated Black people. Melody knows this is true. . . .

She speaks up. "When I went
shopping at Fieldston's with Dwayne,
the manager accused us of stealing,
just because we're Black."

"That's wrong!" her father says.

The grown-ups decide to boycott the store.

Boycotting means not shopping
at the store. It's a way to protest
how the store treats people.
Melody talks to Val and her friends.
They want to boycott the store, too.

Everyone gathers to march.

They lift their voices in protest.

They sing and hold signs.

Melody is proud to speak up

for her rights.

Still, Melody wishes she could make her own change. The next day, she takes her dog, Bo, for a walk to the playground.

It used to be a fun place.

Now there is litter everywhere.

Melody wonders what she can do.

She has an idea to plant a garden
and clean up the playground.

"This is what I can change!"

Melody says.

Melody tells her friends about her plan to fix up the playground and plant a garden. They form a club and elect Melody president. They want to make the park a fun space for the community.

Melody tells her family her plans.

Everyone loves her ideas!

She hopes the park will be ready

in time for the neighborhood's

annual summer picnic.

The work at the playground begins!
Melody and her friends
work hard, but they don't
know how to do everything.
And they are a small group.
Melody worries that she
is not a good president.

Poppa stops by to help.

He encourages Melody.

"A leader doesn't have to do
everything herself," he says.

Melody asks her friends
to bring tools and more kids
to help with the work.

Dwayne asks Melody for help, too.
He wants her to sing on his record!
Dwayne plays the piano as Melody
practices the song. The next day, she
sings the song in a real music studio.

At the playground, more kids come
to help. Melody hums Dwayne's song.
It's catchy! Soon the other kids
are humming it, too.

The week of the picnic,

A big storm hits.

Their hard work is ruined!

Melody is discouraged.

"We were all done,"
she says sadly.
"A garden is never finished,"
Poppa replies. "Gardens
and good works keep going,
but both need tending."

Back home, Melody calls her friends.

They meet in the park,

ready to keep going.

More kids arrive to lend a hand.

With some sunshine
and everyone working together,
the gardens bounce back
and the park gets restored.

On the day of the summer picnic,
the park is as good as new!
Neighbors thank Melody
and her friends
for fixing up the park.

Melody thanks her family and friends
for their support. With their help,
she was able to change her
community as Pastor
Daniels suggested.

Melody and Dwayne perform their song. Her heart is full. She knows she has made a difference.

★ American Girl®
Molly's
Christmas Surprise

by Lauren Clauss
illustrated by Melissa Manwill

Random House 🏠 New York

Meet Molly McIntire!

Molly is a nine-year-old girl who

lives in a small town in 1944.

She is fun, friendly,

and patriotic.

Molly has two brothers

and a sister.

Molly's dad is a doctor
for the army. The United States
is fighting in World War II,
so Dad is in England
taking care of wounded soldiers.

Molly's mom helps with

the war effort at home.

Mom volunteers for the Red Cross.

She also takes care

of the family.

Molly's sister, Jill,
is fourteen
and loves fashion.

Her brother Ricky
is twelve.
He likes to tease.

And Brad is five.

Despite the war, Molly's life
has stayed mostly the same.
She still goes to school
and plays with her friends.
She loves to tap-dance!

But Molly's life has changed
because of the war, too.
Her family—just like every family
in America—has to ration food.
This means they are only allowed
to buy a certain amount
of some foods.

Molly's family grows vegetables
in their backyard.
This way, they don't have to buy
all their food.

Molly is excited for Christmas! She wonders if Dad will send any presents from England. She writes a letter to ask him.

Jill tells Molly

that they may not hear

from their dad.

He is very busy.

Molly knows Jill is right, but she can't help hoping Dad will send something. In her letter, Molly told Dad that she wanted a doll for Christmas. That night, Molly's mom talks to her.

She tells Molly it's never wrong
to hope for good things,
especially at Christmastime.
"Christmas will be different this
year," Mom says. "We'll just
have to make our own surprises!"

The next morning, Molly, Ricky,
and Jill get out the Christmas
decorations. They are
excited to decorate the tree.

But they have to get the tree first!

Since Dad is away

and Mom is shopping with Brad,

the kids combine their money

to buy the tree themselves.

"This is it," Jill says, pointing
to a small, skinny tree.
It's not as pretty and full
as the other trees,
but it costs less.
The piney Christmas smell
cheers Molly up.

CHRISTMAS TREES

"Let's decorate the tree
to surprise Mom and Brad
when they get home!" says Molly.
Once the ornaments and tinsel
are hung, the tree doesn't look
scrawny—it looks beautiful!

The next morning, Molly wakes up
and sees that it has snowed.
Now it really feels like Christmas!
Molly runs outside in her
pajamas to play in the snow.

Ricky opens his window.

He gathers some snow and throws

a snowball at Molly! She laughs.

Jill joins Molly outside,

and the sisters make snow angels

and build snowmen all morning.

At lunchtime, Molly and Jill
head inside. By the front door,
they see a snow-covered package.
It's from Dad! The box says
"Keep Hidden Until Christmas."

"Let's hide it in the garage," Molly says.

Molly and Jill take the box into the garage and cover it with a blanket.

But keeping the box a secret
is hard!

Over the next few days,
Molly makes sure no one
gets too close to it.

Molly is relieved when they
go to the Christmas Eve service.
The secret is safe while everyone
is at church.

Later that night, after everyone
else has gone to bed,
Molly and Jill sneak into
the garage and get the box. They
quietly put it under the tree.

The next morning, everyone is delighted to see the box from Dad! Molly and Jill share a smile and tell the family about the secret. Everyone is glad that the girls saved the box for a special Christmas-morning treat.

KEEP HIDDEN UNTIL CHRISTMAS

The family opens the box,

and everyone gets a present!

Jill gets a new hat.

Ricky gets a silk pilot scarf.

Brad gets a soldier helmet.

Mom gets leather gloves.

And Molly gets a doll
dressed as a nurse.
It is exactly what they each
wanted! At the bottom of the box
is a note telling them
to turn on the radio.

Mom turns on the radio.

The station is playing messages

from servicemen in England.

The family hears

a familiar voice.

It is Dad!

"I'd like to say merry Christmas

to the merry McIntires,"

he says. The family is so happy.

Hearing Dad's voice

is the best gift of all!

When the broadcast is over,

the family starts making

a big Christmas breakfast.

Molly hugs her nurse doll tight.

She is so thankful—even though

her dad is far away, he was

with them on Christmas after all!

☆ American Girl®

Samantha Helps a Friend

by Rebecca Mallary

illustrated by Emma Gillette

Random House 🏠 New York

In the year 1904,

Samantha Parkington lives in

a big house with her grandmother.

She likes to climb trees

and make new friends.

Samantha always tells the truth,

and she will do anything

to help a friend.

Samantha's grandmother,
whom she calls Grandmary, wants
Samantha to be a proper young
lady and practice her embroidery—
but Samantha prefers adventures.
She often scrapes her knees
and tears her stockings!

Grandmary doesn't always approve
of Samantha's fun, but she still
loves her very much.

One of Samantha's favorite
people is her uncle Gard.
Uncle Gard lives in New York City
and has an automobile
that Samantha loves to ride in.
He is the only person
who calls Samantha by
a special nickname: Sam.

Samantha has a neighbor
named Eddie Ryland.
He is always teasing her.
But one day he tells her
something interesting.
There is a new girl next door!

The new girl is Nellie O'Malley,

and she works for Eddie's family.

When Samantha meets Nellie,

she shares a cookie with her

and they become friends.

Nellie has two little sisters, Jenny
and Bridget. Nellie and her sisters
have never been to school
because they had to work.
Now they will get to go
for the first time!

Samantha is excited as she walks
them to their first day of school.
Nellie is nervous, but Samantha
tells her it will be okay.

When Samantha comes to pick up Nellie and her sisters after school, everything is not okay! Nellie is sad. She is crying because the other children teased her for being behind in school. Nellie is in second grade, but others her age are in third grade.

Samantha is sorry

to see her friend so upset,

but she has an idea of how to help!

Samantha sets up a schoolroom
in her house just for Nellie.
She will help Nellie
with reading, writing, and math
so that Nellie can move
to the third grade!

Nellie is happy when she sees
the room with a chalkboard,
books, and beans for counting.
Samantha is glad that Nellie
feels better.

Samantha goes to a school
called Miss Crampton's Academy.
At school, Samantha finds out
that there will be a speech
competition.

Every girl will give a speech
about progress in America.
Two winning girls will get to go
to a bigger competition!

Samantha is not sure what to say
about progress in America.
She decides to ask Grandmary,
Uncle Gard, and the butler,
Mr. Hawkins, about inventions.

Grandmary says the telephone
is the best sign of progress.
Uncle Gard chooses automobiles.
Mr. Hawkins thinks that factories
show America's progress.

Samantha goes to school
with a girl named Edith.
Edith teases Samantha for playing
with a poor girl like Nellie.
Samantha likes Nellie and
doesn't care what Edith says.

The girls give their speeches.
Samantha says that factories
show America's progress because
they make things quickly and
cheaply. She is chosen to go to
the big competition. So is Edith.

Samantha is excited to practice
her speech for Nellie! But
Nellie does not like the speech.
Samantha's feelings are hurt.

She asks Nellie why
she did not like it.
Nellie says it's because
Samantha's speech isn't true.

Nellie used to work in a factory.
She tells Samantha that factories
are dangerous for the children
who work in them.
They have to work all day long
and cannot go to school.
Sometimes they get hurt.

Samantha is surprised.

She did not know what factories

were really like. She wants

her speech to be honest.

At the competition,

Samantha changes her speech.

She talks about what factories

are really like.

She says that to have

real progress in America,

all children need to be safe.

Everyone is shocked, even
Grandmary. But Nellie looks happy.
Then Grandmary claps. Others do,
too. Samantha wins the contest!
She is proud she told the truth.

After the competition, Nellie
has some wonderful news.
Thanks to Samantha's help, she
is moving up to the third grade!
Samantha knew that Nellie
could do it!

Nellie tells Samantha that there is just one problem: in her new class, she sits next to Eddie Ryland!

Samantha promises Nellie
they will keep working hard
so that Nellie can move up
to the front of the class!